To my Thumbuddy:

God loves you so much
You are one of a kind
A blessing from heaven
Whom God has designed

Parents:

As you read this story we encourage you to replace Thumbuddy's name with your child's name.

It was just before bedtime and Mommy sat next to her little Thumbuddy. They closed their eyes and began to pray.

"Thank you Heavenly Father for making my Thumbuddy so precious."

Thumbuddy asked,
"Why am I precious?"

God has given me a precious gift.
~ Genesis 30:20

"You are precious because God loves you. He loves you so much that He made you one-of-a-kind," smiled Mommy.

"Just look at your thumbs. Did you know that you are the only one in the whole world with your thumbprint?"

"The whole world?" Thumbuddy looked at his thumbs, "Look at all my lines and swirls."

God's hands formed you and
made every part of you.
~ Job 10:8

"God made every little swirl and knew
your name, even before you were born."

"God knew me before you and Daddy?
Even when I was in your tummy?"

The Lord called you before your birth; from within the womb He called you by name.
~ Isaiah 49:1

"Oh yes!!" Mommy laughed. "God has always known you and always loved you."

Thumbuddy snuggled with his little dog, "Does God love me as much as I love Paws?"

Nothing will ever separate you from God's love.
~ Romans 8:38-39

"God loves you as much as you love Paws and way, way more! His love is so big that He sent His son Jesus so you and God can be together forever."

"That's a lot. God must think I'm special!"

God so loved the world that He gave His only Son,
so whoever believes in Him shall have eternal life.
~ John 3:16

"That's right! God even knows how many hairs are on your head. He thinks you are special and amazing." Mommy rubbed the top of his head.

"I'm amazing?" asked Thumbuddy.

God knows everything about you and has
even numbered the hairs on your head.
~ Luke 12:7

"Yes," Mommy whispered, "because God is amazing and He made every child one-of-a-kind. He loves all His children."

"Wow!" Thumbuddy smiled.

God loves you and will never quit loving you.
~ Jeremiah 31:3

"Does God love me even when I do something wrong?" asked Thumbuddy.

"God always loves you," said Mommy. "Remember when you got a time out for tracking mud in the house?"

"Yes," Thumbuddy said, "I'm sorry."

Mommy said, "God and I always love you – even when you make a mistake."

The Lord corrects those He loves, just as a
father corrects a child in whom he delights.
~ Proverbs 3:12

"I get it, I get it!" He giggled.
"God loves me just the way I am.
That's why I'm Thumbuddy."

His giggle turned into a silly laugh.

God rejoices over you with singing.
~ Zephaniah 3:17

Thumbuddy and Mommy smiled and touched thumbs – like a new secret handshake.

"You'll always be God's special Thumbuddy, and mine too!"

God will give you hidden treasures, stored in secret places, so you may know that He is the Lord who summons you by name.
~ Isaiah 45:3

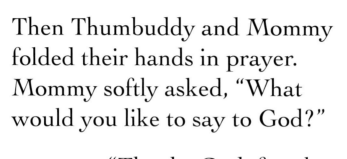

Then Thumbuddy and Mommy folded their hands in prayer. Mommy softly asked, "What would you like to say to God?"

"Thanks God, for always loving me."

"God loves it when we talk with Him," Mommy smiled. "Look at your thumbs again. See how they point to Heaven when you pray?"

If you seek God with all your heart, you will find Him.
~ Deuteronomy 4:29

"Thumbs up, God!" Thumbuddy
said with a big happy smile.

Then his smile slowwwwwly
turned into a yawn.

Blessed are those with pure hearts, for they will see God.
~ Matthew 5:8

Now Thumbuddy was almost too sleepy
to talk. He whispered, "I love you God.
I love you Mommy, Daddy and Paws."

"I will always love my precious you,"
Mommy gently tucked Thumbuddy into bed.

If we love one another, God lives in
us and His love is perfected in us.
~ 1 John 4:12

As Thumbuddy drifted off to sleep Daddy tiptoed into the bedroom. He put his hands on Mommy's shoulders and quietly prayed,

"Thank you God for loving us always and forever. Amen."

Give thanks to the Lord, for He
is good; His love lasts forever.
~ Psalm 107:1

The Salvation Poem

Jesus, You died upon a cross
And rose again to save the lost
Forgive me now of all my sin
Come be my Savior, Lord, and Friend
Change my life and make it new
And help me, Lord, to live for You

About the author:

After my wife, Julie, and I had been married for two years, (at my ripened age of 47), we were blessed to adopt our newborn son, Michael. For the first time in my life, I held a brand-new baby!! As I cradled my precious child, a great wave of love filled my heart and I cried, "You have nothing to worry about because Daddy is here, and I promise I will always love you."

In that very moment, the awe of our Father's love poured over me as God held both Michael and me in his arms and whispered: "I'm here. You too, have nothing to worry about because I love you both and I will love you forever." Eighteen months later, we were blessed again when we adopted our precious newborn daughter, Anica. It was from tears of joy and God's promise to love us that *God Says I'm Thumbuddy* was born.

Visit PositiveKidsBooks.org

God Says I'm Thumbuddy

Little Big Things, Inc.
14400 W Burnsville Pkwy, Burnsville, MN 55306
Thumbuddy and the characters in this book
are copyrights of Little Big Things, Inc.

TheSalvationPoem.com

Library of congress control number: 2011935716
ISBN: 978-0-9801606-8-0

PositiveKidsBooks.org

"See what great love the Father has lavished on us that we should be
called children of God! And that is what we are!" 1 John 3:1

For Julie, Michael and Anica
Thank you for your smiles and love!